Hank Prank
in LOVE

Hank Prank in LOVE

Jules Older

Interior illustrations by Lisa Kopper

AN
APPLE
PAPERBACK

SCHOLASTIC INC.
New York Toronto London Auckland Sydney

ISBN 0-590-43872-7

12 11 10 9 8 7 6 5 4 3 2 1   1 2 3 4 5 6/9

                    Printed in the U.S.A.   42

                First Scholastic printing, May 1991

Contents

Hank Prank in LOVE

1

'Twas the Week before Christmas . . .'

Love crept up on Hank. It hid behind his school desk, and then, when he was least expecting it, banged him on the nut with a tennis racquet. Love hit Hank so hard he saw stars. And planets. And satellites.

It was totally unfair. Hank had just drawn a picture of Mrs Winstone being eaten from the head down by a lion, and from the feet up by a python. He had just written 'Sasquash bites the dust!!!' on the drawing and passed it to Sandeep, who was still chortling to himself, when the classroom door opened. Through the open door, Hank could hear the school choir in Mrs Kapa's room practising for the Christmas pageant.

And the glory,
The glory of the Lord.
And the glory,
The glory of the Lord,
Shall be
Re
Vee
Eel
Ed.

Mr Dunn stepped just inside the door and waited quietly until Mrs Winstone noticed he was there. It took her a while because she was talking excitedly about her favourite subject—the life cycle of the cabbage moth. When she finally saw him, he waited another moment and then spoke to the class in his quiet voice. 'Boys and girls, I want to introduce you to a new student in the school who will also be the newest member of your class. Her name is Lin—L-i-n-h—Tran.

Hank heard him but paid little attention. From next door, the music was growing louder—and more confusing.

And all flesh shall see it together

What?

And all flesh shall see it together

All flesh shall see *what* together? And how can flesh see? Hank tried to picture what the words meant. Hank pictured a big, raw steak with an eye in the middle of it. The picture was revolting.

And all flesh shall see it together,
For the mouth of the Lord hath spoken it.

Mr Dunn continued, 'Linh is from Vietnam. Vietnam is a small country near China. There have been many wars there, and many people have died. Linh is living with foster parents here because her own family was lost in the fighting in Vietnam. She speaks English, but she's a little shy. I know you will make her welcome.'

Hank was paying more attention to the absurd song the choir was singing than to what Mr Dunn was saying about the new class mate.

For the Lord God Omni
Potent Raineth
Hallelujah! Hallelujah!

Mr Dunn beckoned towards the open

door and said, 'Class, I'd like you to meet
Linh Tran.'

Hank's eyes, along with everyone
else's, shifted from Mr Dunn to the
classroom door. A black silk trouser-leg
silently glided through the doorway. The
rest of Linh Tran followed. Her hair hung
long and straight and shiny, shiny black.

It was the black of patent leather shoes and the sleekness of John, the family cat. Her face was round, and her skin was almost gold. What skin! It reminded Hank of the palomino colt whose picture hung over the foot of his bed. Linh's eyes studied the ground; her dark lashes rested lightly on her golden skin.

The door was still open, but now Hank was much more interested in Linh than in the Christmas music.

> And he shall rain for ever and
> Eh
> Ver.

Linh wore clothes like Hank had never seen except on television. Her jacket was made of blue silk with a darker blue pattern. It clung to her from the neck to the waist and had long, tight sleeves. The jacket was slit down the sides from her waist to her knees, and under it Linh

wore loose, black silk trousers. She looked so beautiful that Hank felt dizzy and weak.

The whole time Hank's eyes were locked on his new class mate, Linh's were shyly cast down. Mr Dunn placed his hand lightly on her shoulder and said, 'Linh, I'd like you to meet Mrs Winstone's class.'

Then it happened.

2

Boinnng!

Slowly, s-l-o-w-l-y, Linh raised her long lashes and lifted her gaze. When she did, she looked straight into the scorching eyeballs of Henry Bradley Lawes, also known as Hank Prank. Hank was still staring as hard as he could at Linh. At the spot where their eyes met, there was a sudden *spark* which led to a *sizzle* which turned into a *zap*.

From the room next door, the music thundered.

> Hallelujah!
> Hallelujah!
> Hallelujah!
> HAAA
> LAYYY

LOOOO
YAAA!!!

In that same instant, something SNAPPED in Hank. In the middle of his chest, something twanged like a bow and arrow. It went

BOINNNG!

Suddenly Hank was nothing but Boinng. His knees were Boinng. His fingers were ten quivering Boinngs. 'Boinng' was printed on each eyeball in big, black letters. His poor heart, which had always gone thump-thump, now went Bu-Boinng! Bu-Boinng! Bu-Boinng! It sounded to Hank like the old mantle clock striking a thousand, and he was sure the other kids could hear the appalling din it was making.

Hank's heart wasn't the only part of his body that was making a racket. Something had gone drastically wrong with his breathing. He just couldn't get enough air to his lungs. Every time he breathed in, he heard a sucking sound—

BOINNG BOINNG BOINNG

Every time he breathed out, he heard a blowing sound—

GNNIOB   GNNIOB   GNNIOB

In short, Hank's breathing sounded like a frog who had just hopped up five flights of stairs.

And that wasn't the worst of it.

There were two worsts of it.

The first worst was that Hank felt sure if, by some blessed miracle, Sandeep and Toby and Daniel and Manu were suddenly struck deaf so they couldn't hear what was happening to him, they'd still be able to *see* what was going on. If he felt so goshdarned

BOINNG

then it almost *had* to show. And that would be horrible, because Hank knew he was feeling the one thing which absolutely guaranteed merciless teasing and torment from other boys.

The second worst was that Hank, who that very morning had tied for first in a race to the bus stop, who was the third strongest boy in the class, who could shinny up a rope and touch the ceiling of the gym—that same Hank now felt so weak that he couldn't stand up if he had to. Even sitting, his knees felt like jelly; his arms like they were wearing lead sleeves, while his ten boinnging fingers rattled against each other like castanets.

Hank felt so weak that he couldn't even look around to see if his friends really were staring at him, or if it just felt like they were. It was the longest and awfulest moment of Hank's whole life. And although he hated to admit it even to himself . . . it was also the best. He felt like dying, and he felt like singing. He felt like crawling under his desk, and he felt like dancing on top of it. He felt like running away from class, and most of all, he felt—more strongly than he'd ever felt anything before—like brushing Linh's golden cheek with his own.

Hank had a sudden wish that Sandeep would evaporate, disappear, fall into a black hole, be called to the Principal's office, get flu, go berserk—*anything* to get him out of the seat next to Hank's so that Mr Dunn would send Linh to sit there. But Sandeep looked just as brown and healthy as ever, and Mr Dunn sat Linh in an empty desk near the front between Heather and Malka. All Hank could see of her was her blue silk back with that wonderful hair resting lightly on it.

By the time the bell rang, Hank had regained enough strength to stand up, walk home, climb the stairs, take off his clothes and crawl into bed and under the covers, head and all.

3

Not Hungry

'Honey, where's Hank?' Mr Lawes asked. 'He's never late for fried chicken.'

'Believe it or not, he's in bed. Henrietta, go wake him and tell him supper's ready. I hope he's not getting sick—there's a lot of flu going around.'

Henrietta reluctantly pushed her chair away from the kitchen table and dashed halfway up the stairs. 'Ha-ank! Supper's ready!'

She bounced back down the stairs and was tucking into a drumstick within five seconds. Her mother gave her a severe look and put down the dish of peas she was serving. When she saw that Hank wasn't coming down, she excused herself and went up to see him. During the five minutes she was gone, Henrietta sat with her hands in her lap. Her father sat with his hands in his lap.

When Mrs Lawes returned to the table, they both started to eat, but she didn't join them. 'I don't think he has the flu. He doesn't have a fever, and he's not sick in his stomach. He just says he's not hungry. I wonder if something happened at school. Do you know, Henrietta?'

'Nope,' she answered, reaching for another chicken leg. 'He wasn't in Mr Dunn's office or anything.'

'I'll talk to him after dinner,' Mr Lawes said as he served the rapidly cooling peas to his wife and daughter.

After the meal, he too headed up to Hank's room. Pushing open the door, he saw his son lying very still in bed. Hank's eyes seemed fixed on the picture of the golden colt which was tacked to the wall. He never looked at his father.

'What's the matter, Hank?'

'Nothin'.'

'You sick?'

'No.'

'Stomach hurt?'

'No.'

'You have a fight at school?'

'No.'

'Somebody picking on you?'

'No.'

'Teacher yell at you?'

'No, Dad.'

'Donkey bite you?'

'Dad!'

'Gorilla? Orang-utan? Wild Mouse?'

Hank smiled and glanced at his father. His dad sat on the bed and ran his hand through Hank's hair. 'Tell me, Hank.'

'Oh, I can't. Nothing bad happened,

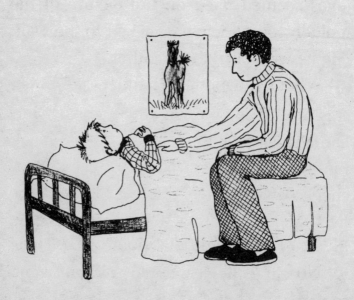

it's just that . . . oh, it's nothing, Dad. I just can't talk about it. I'll be OK.'

Mr Lawes continued to stroke his son's hair. 'OK, Hank,' he said after several more strokes, 'I hope you feel better tomorrow.'

He leaned over and kissed Hank on the forehead. Then he stood up, turned off the light, and left the room, leaving the door open just a crack.

Hank slept from supper-time to break-fast-time, and when he woke up he still felt tired. For a long moment, he couldn't figure out why. Then he opened his eyes, and the first thing he saw was the picture of the palomino. Suddenly it all came crashing back—the Christmas music, Mr Dunn's coming in, Hank's first look at Linh, the way her hair lay against her cheek, that moment his eyes locked on hers, and the feelings that kept exploding in his head for the rest of the day. They were feelings he desperately did not want to name.

But the feelings had a name, and Hank knew what that name was. 'Oh, no,' he groaned, 'not Love. *Anything* but Love!!!'

4

Boys in Love

Why, oh, why is it that boys are allowed to feel anything but love? They can feel angry and nobody minds. They can feel happy and everyone's glad for them. They're allowed to feel lonely and frustrated and bored. It's OK for them to feel silly and stupid. And it's fine to feel heroic and daring and brave.

But love? Oh, no. That's the one thing boys may *not* feel. Love is off-limits; love is taboo. Love is unlawful, illegal, immoral. Love is a drug, a dreg, a drag. Love is for girls.

Fall in love and you're sure to be punished. Not by a judge. Not by the principal. Not even by your parents. Boys who are caught in the grievous crime of falling in love are sentenced without trial by . . . other boys. And the punishment is swift and sure—instant and endless nyaa nyaa-ing from all your male friends until you finally say, 'I hate her! I can't stand her!,' or until you pull some really rotten trick on her to prove you don't care.

Hank knew the rules. In fact, Hank had nyaa-nyaa'd other boys who'd showed only the faintest signs of love, and he'd done so more than once. That only made it worse. Because *now* Hank knew that,

His Turn Had Come.

And that wasn't all that was weighing Hank down before he'd even climbed out of bed. He also had a sneaking worry that when he saw Linh today he wouldn't know what to say or how to walk or what to do with his hands or whether he'd feel like hiding under the desk or tap-dancing on top of it. And he was just a little afraid that if he wanted to dance on the desk, he might just find himself doing it! Then it wouldn't just be Sandeep and Toby and Manu who would torment him. How in the world would he explain it to the rest of the class? And to Sasquash?

The thought of it pushed poor Hank's heavy head back under the covers.

5

Sharks and Hearts

By the time Hank finally pushed back the quilt and climbed out of bed and nibbled at his breakfast and made his way to school, he felt a little better. But when he reached the classroom door, he began feeling dreadful again. Should I go in, he thought, or is there still time to escape? He considered how long it would take to develop a terrible, contagious disease. Too late for that. What about breaking a leg? Then they'd have to take me to hospital. Just as he was wondering where to find a banana skin, he felt a hand push him through the doorway and into the classroom.

'Hi, Hank.'

It was Sandeep.

'What's the matter, Hank?'

'Why's everybody asking me what's the matter?'

'Maybe 'cause you stand around in doorways when everybody's tryin' to get in.'

Hank blushed. He walked over to his seat, sat in it, and pretended not to be looking for Linh Tran. His eyes circled the room and stopped at Linh's desk. But

Linh wasn't there. Hank's heart stopped, then reluctantly started again with a tired, disappointed thump thump . . . thump thump . . . thump thump . . . Where was she?

Mrs Winstone waddled into the room. Out of the corner of his eye, Hank could see Sandeep drawing furiously. From where he sat he could just make out a picture of an extremely fat lady tied to a board, hurtling down a rushing river towards a waterfall. In the pool of water at the base of the falls, shark fins circled.

Hank couldn't even smile. All he wanted to draw was a big, red heart with an arrow through it and two messages carved in it. One would read, HBL LOVES LT. The other would say, LT LOVES HBL.

HBL looked again at LT's desk, but LT was still not there. HBL felt his already heavy heart grow even heavier.

6

Chao Anh

On the playground at recess, Linh still hadn't turned up. Manu and Daniel tried to get Hank to play soccer, and Toby and Sandeep tried to get him to play tag, but he didn't feel like playing anything. So he stood on the sidelines and stared-without-seeing at the kids who were playing.

If he'd really been watching, Hank would have seen the soccer ball coming at him. He would have caught it and kicked it back to the players. But since he wasn't really watching, Hank didn't catch the ball—the ball caught Hank. It caught him square in the middle of the stomach and knocked the wind out of him.

'Oooff!' was all a very surprised Hank Prank could say as he fell backwards to the ground. But he never hit the ground.

Instead, he landed on something soft and slippery. What was it? Or, *who* was it? Hank leapt to his feet and looked.

Oh, no! Oh, *no*! It was Linh he'd knocked over, and the shiny, slippery feeling came from her silk jacket. She looked frightened as she lay there, still not sure what had hit her. Then she saw Hank and lowered her eyes, just as she'd done when Mr Dunn had introduced her to the class. Hank stood there, not knowing what to do. Finally, he reached out his hand. Linh stared at it as if she didn't know what it was. Hank felt himself go red. At last, after what felt like hours, Linh took Hank's hand and let him help her to her feet.

Hank was still in shock from the nearness of her, and the feel of her hand was almost more than he could stand. It felt surprisingly strong and at the same time, soft and warm. Hank was afraid he was going to faint and that Linh would have to help *him* up. He tried to say something but couldn't remember any words.

It was Linh who finally spoke. 'Chao anh,' she said.

'What?'

'Chao anh. That is the way I say hello in Vietnam.'

'Ch-chao—chao what?'

'Chao anh.'

'Oh, chao anh. Hello.'

Linh smiled. 'Chao anh is what girl says

to boy. Boy says, Chao em.'

'Sorry I knocked you down. My name's Hank.'

'Toi ten Linh.'

'Sorry?'

'Toi ten Linh. I am Linh. I am happy to meet you, Hank.'

'Yeah, I know your name. I—uh —heard it when Mr Dunn brought you to class.'

Now Hank gazed at the ground.

'He is very nice man, is he not, Hank?'

'Yeah, he is. He's OK. But not Sasquash.'

'I think I do not know the meaning of sash-cash. Please Hank, what is sash-cash?'

Hank laughed. 'Not sash-cash, Linh. Sasquash! That's what we call Mrs Winstone.'

'What does this word mean?'

'Sasquash is Bigfoot. It's like . . . uh . . . did you ever hear of the

Abdominable Snowman?'

Linh shook her head.

'Well, it means she's big and grumpy.'

'Ah, I know the meaning of grumpy. I shall try very hard not to anger her.'

'You'll be OK. It's mostly boys she picks on.'

The bell rang. Recess was over. Kids poured back into school. It seemed to take only a minute before Hank and Linh were left nearly alone in the playground. 'How do you say hello, Linh? I can't remember.'

'Chao anh, Hank.' And with that, Linh turned and hurried back into the classroom.

Hank was left alone. He felt as light as a balloon, light enough to float back to class. And two thoughts were racing madly through his brain. One was,

I talked to her!
I talked to her!
I talked to her!

The other was,

Chao anh . . .

7

Nyaa—Nyaa

'Hey, Hank!'

Sandeep and Toby and Manu and Daniel were all waiting for him after school.

'How come you didn't wanna' play ball today, Hank?'

'I dunno'. I just didn't feel like it.'

'What *did* you feel like, Hank?'

'Nutthin.'

'Did you feel like talkin' to that new girl?'

'I fell into her.'

'Oh, you fell into her? You just fell into her?'

'Yeah, Linh was standing behind me

when the soccer ball . . .' Hank didn't even have to finish the sentence. He knew he'd made a mistake. The torment began for real.

'Linh! Linh! How'dya' know her name's Linh, Hank?'

'Mr Dunn said—'

'Maybe you asked her, Hank.'

'What if I—'

'Maybe you *begged* her, Hank?'

'I didn't beg—'

'Maybe you LOVE her, Hank!'

'I . . . I . . .'

'Hank loves Li-inh,
Hank loves Li-inh,
Nyaa, na-na, nyaa na,
Hank loves Linh!'

Hank turned as red as a ripe tomato. He had a horrible choice to make. He could tell his mates that he couldn't stand the sight of Linh, and they'd leave him alone. Or he could say nothing and be tormented and teased for the rest of his life. The choice was absolutely Abdominable.

8

Do You Love Her?

'All right, you guys, you listen to me—'

'We're listening, Hankie, Got yer' hankie, Hankie?'

'You're not listening, you're—'

'We're all ears, Hankie. Tell us what it's like to be in love. You are in love, aren't you, Hankie?'

'Yes.'

'You are so in . . . what?'

'Yes.'

'We asked you if you were in love.'

'And I said, "yes".'

'Hank, do you understand what we're asking you?'

'You want to know if I'm in love.'

'Then you admit it?'

'Yes.'

'Yes, what, Hank?'

'Yes, I am in love.'

'*Oh, no!*'

'I'm in love with Linh.'

There was a long, long, *long* silence. Manu looked at Toby. Toby looked at Sandeep. Then they all stared at Hank. This wasn't going right. None of them could think of what to say next.

So Hank spoke again. 'Do you really want me to tell you what it's like to be in love?'

More silence. Finally, Sandeep said, 'I do.'

Hank nodded to Toby. 'What about you?'

Toby blushed. 'If you wanna'.'

'If I wanna' *what*, Toby?'

'Uh, if you wanna' tell us what it's like to . . . uh . . . be in you-know, I'll . . . uh . . . listen.'

'Manu?'

'OK by me, Hank. What's it like?'

'Let's go up the hill, and I'll tell you.'

The four of them trudged up Ravensbourne Hill until they came to a grassy place where they could look down on the school, on their houses, on the harbour.

They threw their backpacks down and flopped on top of them. 'C'mon, Hank, tell us about it.'

'About what, Manu?'

'About bloomin' being in bloomin' love!'

'OK, it's like this . . .' They all settled down into the grass, their heads on their packs.

'You know when Mr Dunn brought Linh to class. Well, as soon as I saw her, somethin' happened. It was like everything went BOINNG. I thought maybe I'd had a heart attack. Or maybe it was like getting hit by a train. Whatever it was, it

almost knocked me over. Right from then, I knew I loved her.'

Toby whistled softly.

'It was great, and it was terrible too. Everything was going Boinng, Boinng, Boinng, and it felt crazy and fantastic, but I was afraid you guys would spot it, and you'd tease me.'

'Hey, we wouldn't do that, Hank.'

'Yeah, whaddaya' take us for?'

'Yeah, Hank, we're your friends. Anyway, tell us more.'

'Well, it's just this great feeling. Like I can't stop smiling. And I feel like I could fly. It's just . . . I don't know, it's just love.'

'It sounds brilliant! Does Linh love you?'

'I don't know. And don't you ask her either!'

9

New Gear

After their talk, the boys stopped teasing Hank about love. In fact, Manu started mooning around Heather, and even Toby showed occasional signs of interest in girls.

Christmas came and went, with only one difference from last year and the year before. This time, instead of dreading the day school would start again, Hank couldn't wait for it. When it finally arrived, he was out of the house before Henrietta had even finished her breakfast cereal.

Hank had decided the night before that he'd be the first kid at school, and he wasn't far from it. Alistair Llewellyn-Jones was sitting on the school steps reading a maths book (a *maths* book!), and two or three other sleepy looking kids were wandering around the playground, but aside from them, Hank had the place to himself. This is weird, he thought. I've

never seen the place so empty. The teachers aren't even here yet. Definitely weird with no teachers around and with no Sandeep around and with no . . .

Hank didn't say the name, but despite what he'd done just before falling asleep, Linh wasn't there. What he'd done was to beam his thoughts as hard as he could towards Linh's house. With his eyes screwed shut, he'd sent out one message in her direction. The message was,

'Meet Hank at school.'
'Meet Hank at school.'
'Meet Hank at school.'
'Meet Hank at school.'

Hank sat on one of the playground swings and closed his eyes as tight as he could. 'Meet me now, Linh. Meet me now.'

A slight movement of air brushed against Hank's face. He opened his eyes, but everything looked blurry. Someone

was standing in front of him. As his eyes
came back into focus he could see that the

someone had dark hair, that the someone
was a girl, and that the someone was
looking at him. His heart stopped. Then it
went

Bu-Boinng! Bu-Boinng! Bu-Boinng!

It had to be Linh. She'd heard his message! Telepathy Rules Hooray! But as Hank's eyes cleared, he saw that the dark-haired girl before him wore her hair in braids. And instead of a silk suit, she wore jeans and a red shirt. She *looked* like Linh but she didn't *dress* like Linh.

'Hello, Hank. I am wishing you a Happy New Year.'

'Uh . . .'

'And I am wishing you a Merry Christmas.'

'Uh . . .'

'Do you like the fine clothing my foster parents gave me for Christmas, Hank?'

'Linh?'

'Do you not know me?'

'Uh, sure. Sure I know you.'

Hank did not know her. And now that he did know her, he still did not know her. She looked so different without her

Vietnamese clothes that it was almost like looking at a different person.

'Do you not like my new clothing, Hank? Am I wearing something that is wrong? Please tell me before we go to our class. I will be ashamed if I am wearing wrong clothing.'

'No, no Linh. The clothes are OK. Everybody wears jeans. And you're wearing them just right. You look good in them.'

'But I think you are not pleased. Is this so? Please tell me.'

'It's not . . . I'm . . . no, well, I . . .'

Words were coming out of Hank's mouth, but none of them made any sense. He tried again.

'You look nice, Linh. It's just that . . . what I mean is . . .'

'Do you prefer my *ao dai* to jeans, Hank?'

'*Ao dai*?'

'My Vietnamese clothing.'

'Yes. I love it.' Hank couldn't believe what he'd just heard coming out of his own mouth. He couldn't believe it even more when his mouth kept on talking. 'I love the way it looks on you. I . . . love . . . the way it looks on you. Linh, I think it . . . I . . .'

The schoolbell rang. Other kids started to race towards the door. Linh stood very still. Hank sat very still.

'Yes, Hank?'

'I love you there's the bell let's go or Sasquash will kill us see you inside bye now I gotta run Sandeep's waiting for me see you later goodbye.'

10

Do You Love Me?

Over the next few weeks Hank and Linh sometimes met before school and sometimes after. She got to know Toby and Manu and Sandeep, and they got friendlier with her best friends, Malka and Heather. Linh always wore jeans and shirts now, which was nice, but when Hank dreamily thought about her, as he did almost every night before drifting into sleep, she was always wearing her *ao dai*. And in his dreams, her long black hair was never in braids but fell onto her silken shoulders just as it did on her first day in class.

Hank no longer felt his heart gallop and

his fingers rattle whenever he saw Linh, but if he was less in boinng, he was more in friendship. Still, there were a couple of things he felt sorry about. He'd never pressed his cheek against hers. And although he'd told Linh he loved her, she had never said she loved him back.

Hank had hinted to her that he'd like to know, but she didn't seem to get the hint. One day he'd hinted so much that she finally did say something, but it wasn't the something he was expecting. 'Hank, you are good friend for whom I care. But please do not ask me about love. In Vietnam a boy would never ask a girl such a question, and if he did, a girl would never answer.'

'But we're not in Vietnam, we're in . . .'

'Hank! This is how my parents would have me behave if they were . . .' Linh took a deep breath. A small tear formed in the corner of each eye. She spoke slowly, forcing herself to say the words. 'If my parents were still alive, they would not wish me to discuss such things. I am sorry, Hank.'

11

Something Happened!

It was on a Tuesday afternoon that Mr Dunn came again to Mrs Winstone's class. As he whispered quietly to her, she looked surprised at what he was saying. In her louder whisper, she asked, 'Are you sure?'

Mr Dunn nodded and whispered some more. Then he turned to the class, looked between Heather and Malka, and said, 'Linh, I'd like to talk to you. Will you please come with me?'

The beautiful golden colour in Linh's face drained away. Her shoulders tensed and her knuckles went white as she gripped the sides of her desk. She took a deep breath, then slowly rose and walked to the front of the room.

The class was absolutely silent. Hank wanted to run to Linh, to protect her, to throw his arms around her. But it was Mr Dunn who placed his hand on Linh's shoulder and guided her out the door and towards his office. Mrs Winstone started talking about geography again and kept talking about it until the end-of-the-day bell rang. Linh had still not come back.

Hank and Sandeep started down the corridor towards the playground, but just before they got to the school door, Hank stopped suddenly. 'You go on without me.'

'What's the matter, Hank?'

'I—uh—forgot something. See ya tomorrow.'

Hank walked back in the direction of their classroom, but as soon as he turned the corner, he raced to Mr Dunn's office and looked in the door.

Mr Dunn's secretary was on one phone, and the other phone was ringing. In the corner of the room, a man with a flash camera was arguing with a woman. Neither of them were teachers. Mr Dunn wasn't there. And neither was Linh.

Something's happened to Linh! I know it, I just know it. But what can I do? She's not here, so maybe . . . I know! She might be at home. I'll go and see.

Hank dashed through the corridors, flew out the door, raced across the play-ground, and ran towards the house where Linh and her foster parents lived. It took him only five minutes to get there, but he'd run so hard that his heart was thumping and his lungs felt like they were exploding. He leaned against her gate. The door to Linh's house was shut, but through the curtains Hank could see people moving inside. He couldn't see Linh.

Hank tried to make himself march up to the door and pound on it, but he just couldn't do it. Instead, he waited. And waited.

After leaning on the gate for what seemed forever with no sign of the door opening, Hank finally decided to call it quits. He had to go home. He turned toward the street—then stopped dead in his tracks. For the first time he noticed the two station wagons and the truck that were parked in front of Linh's house. All three had white lettering painted on their doors. One said 'Daily Times'. The other said, 'Radio News Team'. And on the truck was printed a familiar eye and the words, 'Television News'.

What was going on?

12

News Flash

As he walked home, Hank tried and tried to make sense of the afternoon. Mr Dunn's visit . . . Sasquash's surprise . . . Linh's disappearance . . . the man with the camera . . . and now these news people at Linh's house. His head was swimming, and the more he thought, the more he started to drown.

When Hank got home, all he wanted to do was go to bed, something he hadn't done before supper since the day Linh Tran was introduced to his class—and to his life. And to bed he went, without dinner and with his head buried under the covers. Like the last time, a heavy,

heavy feeling weighed down on him.

But this time something different happened. It happened just after supper was over. From his bed, Hank could hear the TV and knew his parents would be watching the news. Then he heard his father calling, 'Hank! Come down! There's somebody from your school on the news.'

Hank leapt out of bed and pulled on his pants. Not bothering with shoes or socks, he dashed down the steps, struggling to get his shirt on.

By the time he reached the bottom he'd managed to force his arms through the sleeves. He was still trying to find the hole for his head when the doorbell rang. Hank couldn't find the blasted hole, much less the door. He butted around until he finally broke through to daylight just in time to see his parents open the door. Standing on the front porch were a man and woman. 'Mr and Mrs Lawes?'

'Yes.'

'Hi. Sorry to disturb you. I'm Basil James, and this is my wife, Gerry. We're the family that's looking after Linh Tran, one of Hank's class . . .'

'We were just watching her on the news. It's simply amazing, isn't it.'

Hank couldn't believe his ears. Linh's family! But what was amazing, and *what* was going on? He blurted out, 'Is Linh all right?'

'This must be Hank.'

'Yes. Sorry. Henry, this is Mr and Mrs James, your class mate's foster . . .'

Hank couldn't wait. 'I know. I know. But what I don't know is whether Linh's all right?' He was nearly crying.

'Hasn't Hank heard the. . . ?'

'Sorry, Mr James. I forgot. Hank didn't see the news.'

'IS SHE ALL RIGHT?'

'I am all right, Hank.'

That voice! Mr and Mrs James stepped

apart, and there, right behind them, stood Linh. She wore the same Vietnamese clothes she'd worn that first day at school, and her hair flowed like a black waterfall onto her shoulders.

Hank couldn't believe his eyes.

13

Vinh Biet Anh

The six of them stood around the front door; none of them spoke. Finally, Mrs James cleared her throat and said, 'Ahem. Mr and Mrs Lawes, I believe that Linh and Hank would like to talk together. Perhaps we could . . .'

Mrs Lawes looked at her son and then at the beautiful stranger she'd seen on television just minutes before. 'Of course,' she answered. 'Why don't we adults step outside? It's a lovely night.'

The parents stepped out on the porch, and Linh joined Hank in the hallway. Hank's mother closed the door between the four adults and the two kids. Hank was still in shock. He gazed at Linh for a long time. Then, almost in tears, he begged her: 'Tell me . . . *please* . . . what's going on?'

'Hank, I have important news.'

'What is it?'

'Mr Dunn came to tell me that my

mother and my older brother have been located. They are alive! I do not know about my father or my sisters, but my mother and brother are alive!'

'Oh! Oh! That's . . . that's great!'

'It is wonderful.'

'Where are they?'

Linh looked down at the carpet. 'That is not wonderful.'

Hank waited.

'My mother and my brother are in a place named Maryland. I think it is far away.'

'Oh, no! Does that mean . . .' Hank's voice trailed off.

'I leave early tomorrow morning to join them in Maryland.'

They both stood silent for a long time. Finally, Linh spoke again. 'I shall miss this place. I shall miss my foster parents who have been so kind to me.' A tear rolled down her cheek. 'I shall miss my new friends.' She shed another tear. 'And most of all, Hank, I shall miss you.'

Tears now rolled down Hank's cheeks too. He started to brush them away but stopped, reached out and lightly clasped Linh's shoulders. He felt her tremble. He felt himself trembling too. Hank leaned towards Linh and gently brushed his tear-streaked cheek against hers. The feeling was just as soft and beautiful as he'd imagined it would be.

'I love you, Linh.'

'I love you too, Hank. And now I must say, vinh biet anh.'

Hank had never heard the words before, but he knew what they meant.

They meant farewell.

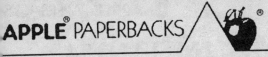

THE BABY-SITTERS CLUB®

Collect Them All!

by Ann M. Martin

The seven girls at Stoneybrook Middle School get into all kinds of adventures...with school, boys, and, of course, baby-sitting!

For a complete listing of all the Baby-sitter Club titles write to:
Customer Service at the address below.

Available wherever you buy books...or use this order form.

Scholastic Inc., P.O. Box 7502, 2931 E. McCarty Street, Jefferson City, MO 65102

Please send me the books I have checked above. I am enclosing $ _____
(please add $2.00 to cover shipping and handling). Send check or money order — no cash or C.O.D.s please.

Name _____

Address _____

City _____ State/Zip_____

Please allow four to six weeks for delivery. Offer good in U.S.A. only. Sorry, mail orders are not available to residents of Canada. Prices subject to change.

BSC790

SLEEPOVER FRIENDS™
by Susan Saunders

APPLE PAPERBACKS

THE GYMNASTS™

by Elizabeth Levy